To Mom and Dad, who helped make
this kid's wishes come true. —SB

Published by Disney Press, an imprint of Buena Vista Books, Inc. No part of this book may be reproduced
or transmitted in any form or by any means, electronic or mechanical, including photocopying, recording,
or by any information storage and retrieval system, without written permission from the publisher. For
information address Disney Press, 1200 Grand Central Avenue, Glendale, California 91201.

Designed by Winnie Ho
Printed in the United States of America
First Hardcover Edition, October 2023
10 9 8 7 6 5 4 3 2 1
FAC-034274-23229
ISBN 978-1-368-09365-1

Library of Congress Control Number: 2023936515

For more Disney Press fun, visit www.disneybooks.com

Inspired by

Disney

WISH

The Grateful Goat

Written by **Steve Behling**

Illustrated by **Annette Marnat**

Disney PRESS

Los Angeles • New York

Valentino the goat lives in Rosas, the Kingdom of Wishes, where anything is possible.

Valentino has important things to say—and he says them loudly. But no one, including his friend Asha, can understand what he wants.

"What was that?" Asha asks Valentino. "Oh, I don't speak goat."

"Perhaps he'd like you to draw him in your journal," suggests Asha's grandfather Sabino.

Asha finishes the drawing and shows it to Valentino.

What is he trying to say?

aaaaaaa!

Maaaaaaa!

"I know what Valentino wants," says Sakina, Asha's mother. "He needs pajamas to keep him warm!"

So she dresses Valentino in some very cute pajamas. "What else could he want?" Asha wonders.

Maaaaaa! Maaaaaaa

Maaaaaaa!

Maaaaaaa!

Valentino follows Asha to visit Dahlia, a friend who works in the castle kitchens.

"Do you have any idea what Valentino could want?" asks Asha.

Dahlia knows a *lot* about baking. But she does not know much about goats.

"Hmm," Dahlia says. "Maybe he's hungry.
Would you like a cookie, Valentino?"

The goat nibbles on the cookie.

Valentino wants to tell Dahlia something. But what is it?

Dahlia's friends try to help. Hal thinks honey might calm Valentino. Safi offers him a handkerchief. But the little goat continues raising a ruckus.

Simon snoozes despite the noise. Not even Valentino can wake him up!

Maaaaaaa!
Maaaaaaa!
Maaaaaaa!

Dario acts silly to entertain Valentino. Bazeema whispers a compliment in his ear.

But Valentino has more to say!

Gabo scowls and covers his ears. **"What more could he want?"** he asks.

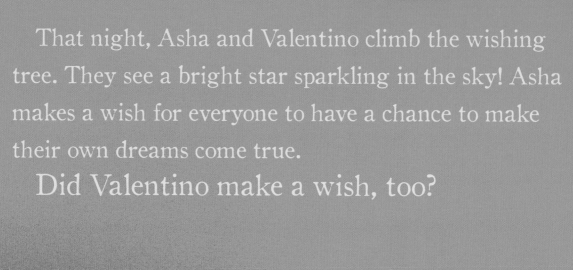

That night, Asha and Valentino climb the wishing tree. They see a bright star sparkling in the sky! Asha makes a wish for everyone to have a chance to make their own dreams come true.

Did Valentino make a wish, too?

Maaaaaaa!

Maaaaaaa!

Asha's wish brings down a real star from the sky! Star sprinkles Valentino with stardust. The little goat opens his mouth to say something—and *words* come out!

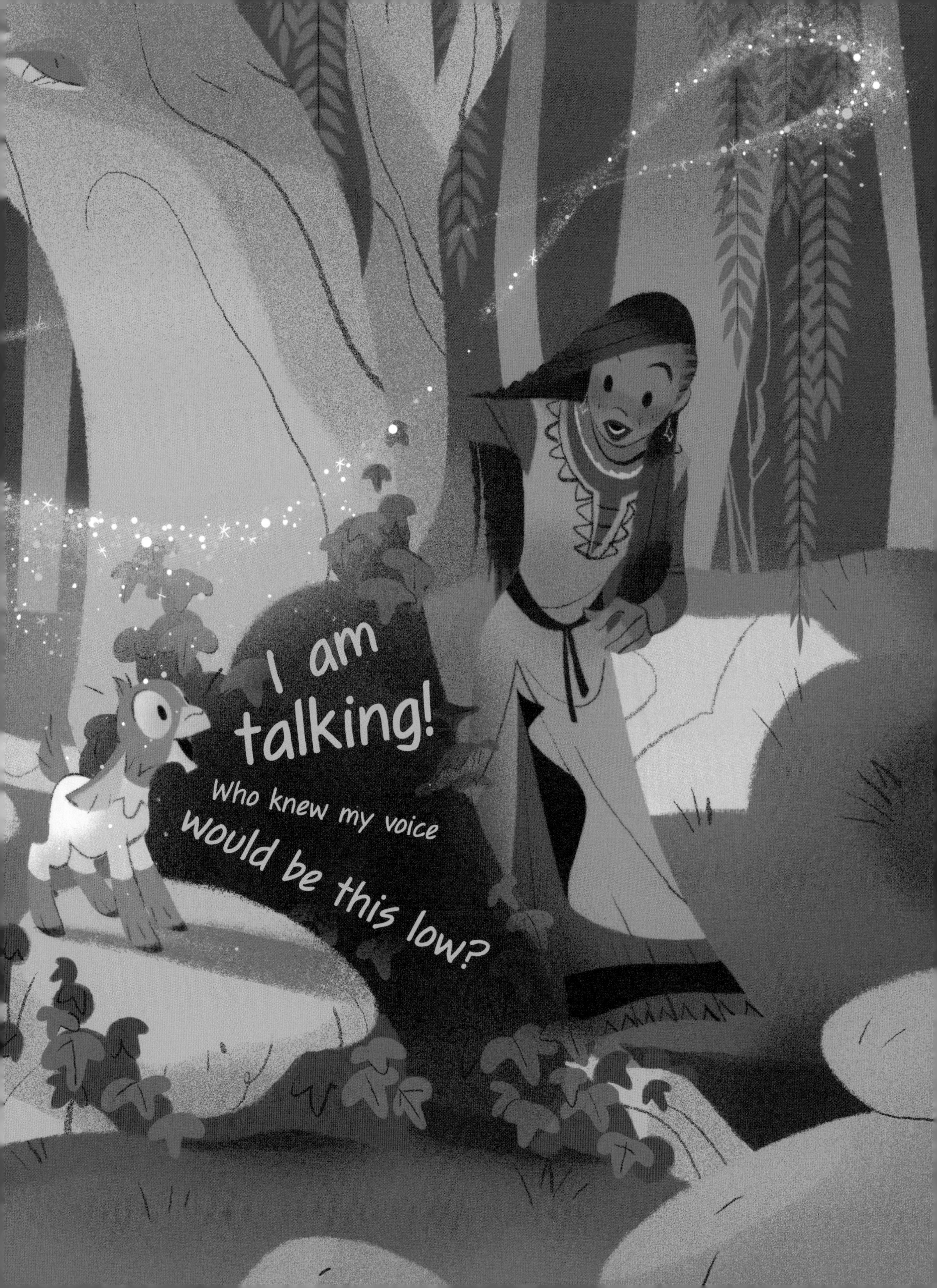
I am talking!
Who knew my voice would be this low?

Star sprinkles stardust on the mushrooms,
the bunnies, and a turtle so they can speak, too.
Valentino wants to talk to *everyone*!

Oh, this is
fantastic!

Asha thinks the world might
not be ready for a talking goat,
so she hides Valentino and Star
in the chicken room while she
figures out what to do. Valentino
is less than thrilled.

"I'll be right back," Asha
promises. "Stay quiet."

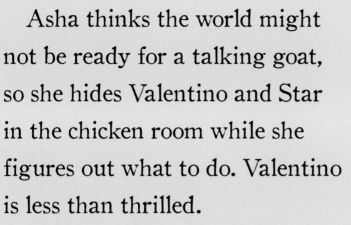

With the chickens?
No! Did you see
what just came out
of that one's b—

But Valentino will not be silenced!
Star sprinkles the room with stardust. Soon Valentino
is conducting a choir of singing chickens!

Your wings can't fly,
but your voices can!

The chickens thank Valentino for bringing them so much joy. In that moment, Valentino remembers *why* he wished for a voice in the first place. . . .

It was so he could finally say thank you to all of his friends!
But there's no time to waste. He has *a lot* of gratitude to share!

First Valentino thanks Dahlia for the delicious treats.

Your cookies taste way better than hay.

He tells the teens that he's grateful for their friendship.

Even you, Gabo.

Next Valentino tells Sakina he loves his new pajamas.
Not only do they keep him warm, but they are *very* stylish!
Then he thanks Asha for the beautiful drawing she
made of him.

Of course, it helps that you had such a handsome subject.

It's time for Star to return to the sky. Before Star leaves, Valentino says thank you to his new friend.

Because of you, everyone finally understands me.

Star gives Asha a special wand to keep its magic in Rosas. Valentino's magnificent voice is here to stay!

Valentino is happy. He promises to use his voice to be kind to others. . . .

And to say **thank you** to all my friends.

Thank YOU!
Thank YOU!